maybe it's because I'm a Londoner...

**A ROOM
IN MY HOUSE**
design.make.produce.

www.aroominmyhouse.com

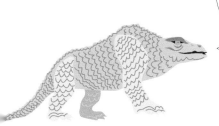

Published independently by
A Room in my House Ltd
www.aroominmyhouse.com

ABC of ANIMALS in London
A Completely Unpredictable Menagerie
Copyright © A Room in my House 2016
Text copyright © A Room in my House 2016
Illustrations copyright © A Room in my House 2016
Written, illustrated, designed and compiled by Cristina Guidone-Charles

ISBN 978-0-9935978-0-0

Printed by Dolman Scott Ltd. Designed in North London.

ABC for Eva

of ANIMALS in London

a completely unpredictable menagerie

Cristina Guidone-Charles

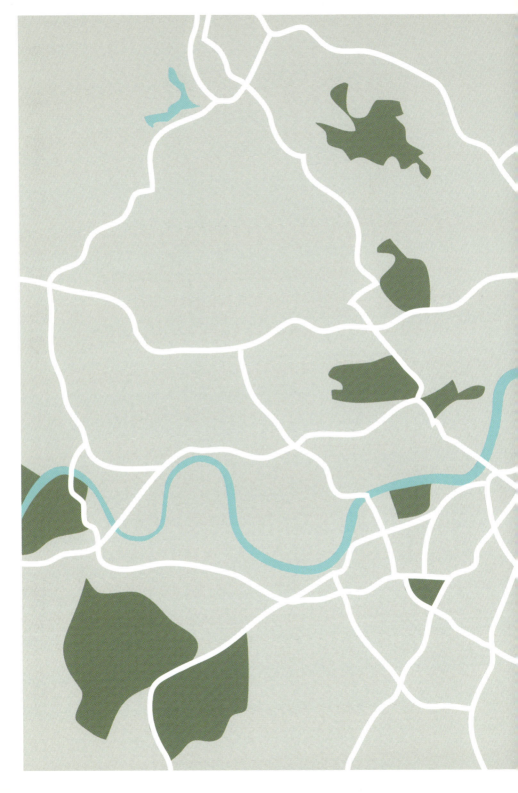

WELCOME TO LONDON.

This city has been my home since the day I was born,
and although no-one who knows me would call me
an animal-lover, I most certainly am a London-lover!

However, that said, with such a passion for my home city
it soon became clear that animals did seem to appear
as a recurring theme throughout London's history.

And let's face it there's nothing like a cute furry animal
to pull in the crowds although, to be fair, there aren't
many animals of the cute and furry variety that are about
to be revealed in the next 60 pages!

But as a graphic designer with 20 professional years under
my belt I urge you to turn the page, enjoy the illustrations
that have been an absolute joy to produce, and marvel
at 26 fascinating stories that have been both intriguing
to discover and challenging to get factually correct.

London, animals and the ABC are about
to get a whole lot more interesting...

Cristina

A is for ant

Summer 2014 saw a North London home infested by Asian super ants known to chomp through electrical cables triggering house fires. This was the first time this rare breed had been found in London.

 is for bee

In 2014 a swarm of honey bees descended upon
the window of high street fashion chain, Topshop.
The Victoria Street store window soon became a wall
of bees as the Queen Bee's devoted colony followed
her to this unusual nesting place.
Later that day, after being safely smoked into a box,
the colony was moved to the Westminster cathedral
apiary to be looked after by beekeepers.

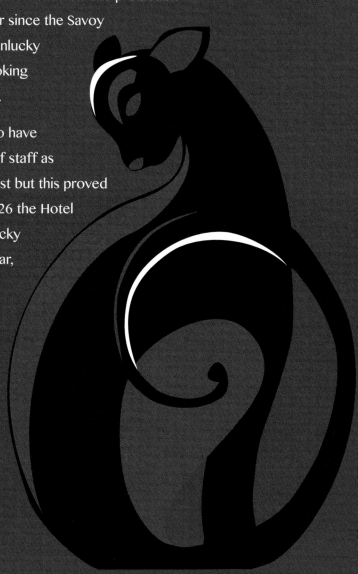

In 1898 a business man booked a table for fourteen at the
Savoy Hotel. At the last minute one of the guests cancelled;
another guest remarked how unlucky this was and that
the last person to leave the table of thirteen would
be the first to die. Six weeks later the prediction
came true and ever since the Savoy
has considered it unlucky
to have a table booking
for thirteen guests.

The solution was to have
a Savoy member of staff as
the fourteenth guest but this proved
unpopular so in 1926 the Hotel
commissioned a lucky
black cat and Kaspar,
a 2ft high art deco
sculpture, was
the result.

To this day
he is seated as
the fourteenth
guest at every
table that has
been booked
for thirteen!

is for Cat, Kaspar the cat

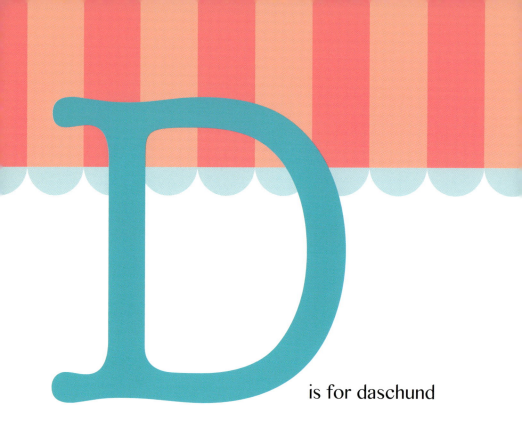

D

is for daschund

In 2013 sausage-dog-mad-Londoner Emilie Harley attempted to raise £55,000 through crowd funding to open the pooch-friendly Sausage Dog Cafe in Brixton. It never opened. Only £1,500 was raised.

E is for elephant

2010 brought an Elephant Parade to the capital.
The brightly painted model elephants found in London's parks,
streets and tourist attractions were then auctioned and raised
over £4 million for the Elephant Family Charity, a conservation
movement registered in 2002 which exists to save the endangered
Asian elephant from extinction in the wild.

is for flamingo

100ft above street level, on top
of a department store in Kensington, you'll find
the Kensington Roof Gardens established in the 1930s
with resident flamingoes.

Guy the Gorilla arrived at London Zoo
on 5 November 1947 (Guy Fawkes night!).
For over 30 years he was one of the
Zoo's most popular attractions, so
popular in fact, that after his death in 1978
the Zoo commissioned a larger-than-life
sculpture of Guy to stand
by the main entrance.

is for guy the gorilla

is for horse

Jacob, the Circle dray horse

The famous Courage dray horses were stabled
on this site* from the early nineteenth century and
delivered beer around London from the brewery
on Horselydown Lane by Tower Bridge.

In the sixteenth century the area became known
as Horselydown, which derives from 'horse-lie-down',
a description of working horses resting before
crossing London Bridge into the City of London.

Jacob (*a life-size statue*) was commissioned by Jacobs
Island Company and Farlane Properties as the centrepiece
of the Circle to commemorate the history of the site.

He was flown over London by helicopter into Queen
Elizabeth Street to launch the Circle in October 1987.

**The Circle, completed by architects in 1990,
is a development of apartments, shops and offices clad
in striking blue glazed bricks, once the stables for
London's beer delivering Courage dray horses.*

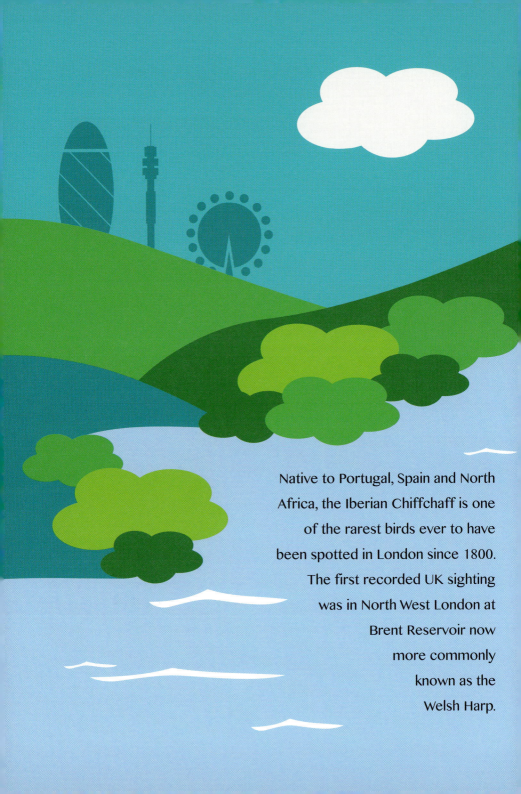

Native to Portugal, Spain and North Africa, the Iberian Chiffchaff is one of the rarest birds ever to have been spotted in London since 1800. The first recorded UK sighting was in North West London at Brent Reservoir now more commonly known as the Welsh Harp.

is for Iberian chiffchaff

J is for jellyfish

Based in Forest Hill, the Horniman Museum's aquarium is one of London's oldest surviving aquaria. Frederick Horniman is said to have been inspired to construct an aquarium in the Museum after viewing the Aquarium at the Great Exhibition in the Crystal Palace, Hyde Park, 1851.

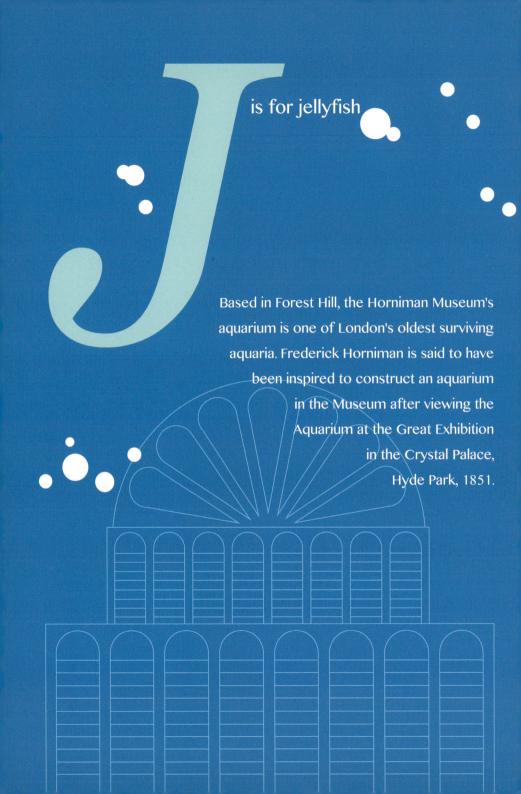

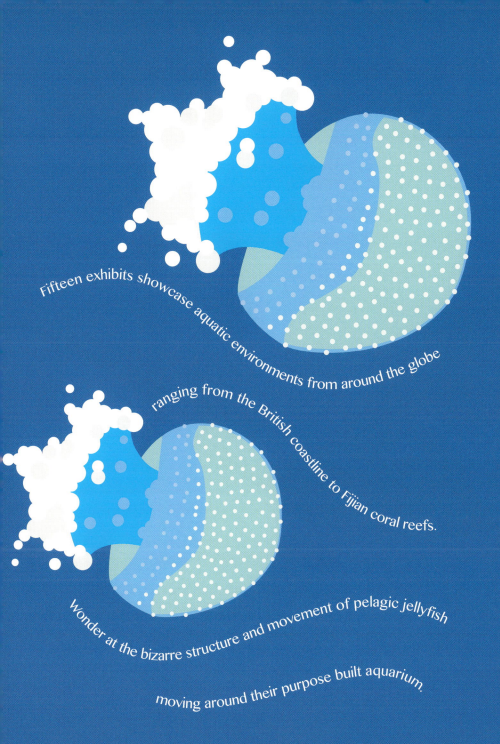

Fifteen exhibits showcase aquatic environments from around the globe

ranging from the British coastline to Fijian coral reefs.

Wonder at the bizarre structure and movement of pelagic jellyfish

moving around their purpose built aquarium.

In 2007
the British
Waterways wildlife
survey focused
on the kingfisher.
London had 39 spottings,
higher than any other urban area.
Ecologists pinpointed Regent's Canal between City Road Basin,
Islington and Old Ford Lock in Tower Hamlets
as the best place to spot a kingfisher.
This is great news for Londoners as kingfisher sightings
are generally accepted as a key indicator of good
quality water and a healthy ecosystem.

K

is for kingfisher

From 1869-1870 lions heads were sculpted along both sides of the Thames Embankment.

The saying goes:
"When the lions drink, London will sink";
these lions were London's flood warning system.
If the river level reached the top of the lions heads London was in danger of flooding.

L
is for lion

The Crystal Palace Dinosaurs were commissioned
in 1852 to accompany the Crystal Palace after its move
from the Great Exhibition in Hyde Park and unveiled
in 1854; they were the first dinosaur sculptures in the world.

Although considered varyingly inaccurate by modern
standards, the models were designed and sculpted by Benjamin
Waterhouse Hawkins using the latest scientific knowledge.

The Megalosaurus became one of the park's three 'mascot
dinosaurs' along with the Iguanodon and the Ichthyosaurus.

The models were classed as Grade II listed buildings
from 1973, extensively restored in 2002, and upgraded
to Grade I listed in 2007.

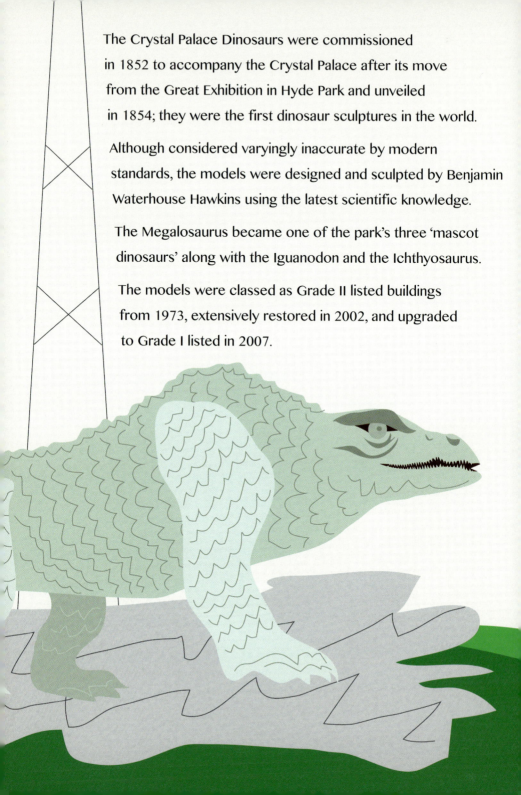

is for megalosaurus

A colony of endangered newts were relocated for the 2012 Olympics at a cost of £70,000.

By law the London Development Agency had to move the great crested newts to allow for the development of the Olympic Velopark in Stratford, east London.

They didn't have to move far though, these protected creatures found a safe new home within the Olympic facility in Hog Hill.

is for newt, great crested

O

is for ostrich

It all started with King Henry III receiving a gift of 3 lions;
in 1236 the Royal Menagerie at the Tower of London was opened.

Over the course of the next 600 years it housed animals such
as a polar bear that fished in the Thames, an African elephant
that drank red wine in the winter, a pipe smoking baboon
and an ostrich that was fed over 100 iron nails.

It died!

In 1835, on the orders of the Duke of Wellington the animals were
moved to their new home in Regent's Park, London Zoo.

is for penguin

In 1934 London Zoo unveiled its famous spiral-ramped 'Penguin Pool' designed by Tecton, an influential architectural firm led by Russian emigre Berthold Lubetkin.

Tecton's innovative Modernist design was unusually elegant and playful and one of the first uses of reinforced concrete.

During a refurbishment in 2004 the penguin colony was temporarily relocated to one of the zoo's duck ponds. The penguins took such a strong liking to their new habitat that it was decided that they would remain there.

The Penguin Pool is now registered as Grade I listed.

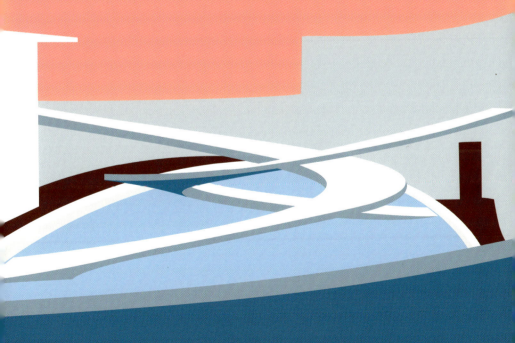

The quagga, extensively hunted for its skin in the 19th century, is an extinct subspecies of the plains zebra with origins in South Africa.

Although there are 23 known stuffed and mounted quagga specimens in museums throughout the world, the only photographs of a living quagga were taken at London Zoo between 1863 and 1870.

This mare died in 1872. The last captive specimen, a female, died in an Amsterdam zoo in August 1883.

is for quagga

The infamous ravens of the
Tower of London are known worldwide
and legend has it that the Kingdom will
fall if ever the ravens are to leave the Tower.

Since the reign of Charles II a Raven
Master has been appointed to ensure
the ravens stay within the Tower's
boundaries. Enrolled as soldiers
of the Crown, just as human
members of the armed
forces, the ravens can
be dismissed for
unsatisfactory
conduct.

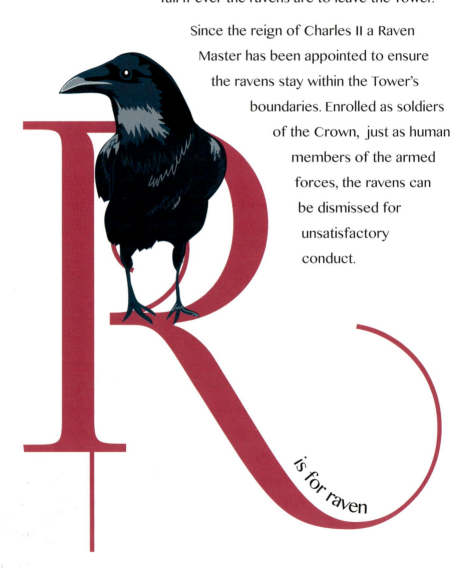

is for raven

Raven George was dismissed for eating television aerials.

Raven Grog was last seen outside an East End pub!

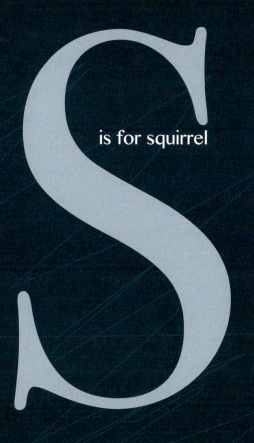

S is for squirrel

Frank Buckland, a Victorian surgeon, zoologist, author and natural historian, was a pioneer of zoophage: eating animal flesh in the name of science.

In London, 1859 he formally set up the Acclimatisation Society to explore the possibilities of introducing exotic flora and fauna into the British wilderness whilst furthering the search for new food.

Dinner party menus regularly included boiled elephant trunk, porpoise heads, stewed mole, mice in batter and squirrel pie.

Upon the death of George I in 1727, George II
and his new Queen, Caroline, moved into Kensington Palace
inheriting a menagerie within the palace grounds.

The resident Bengal tigers, housed in iron dens,
ate up to 200 kilos of meat each week!

Although apparently the King remained content with snails
(that would later become his dinner), the Queen's now highly
favoured collection of animals was moved to the
Tower Menagerie before her death in 1737.

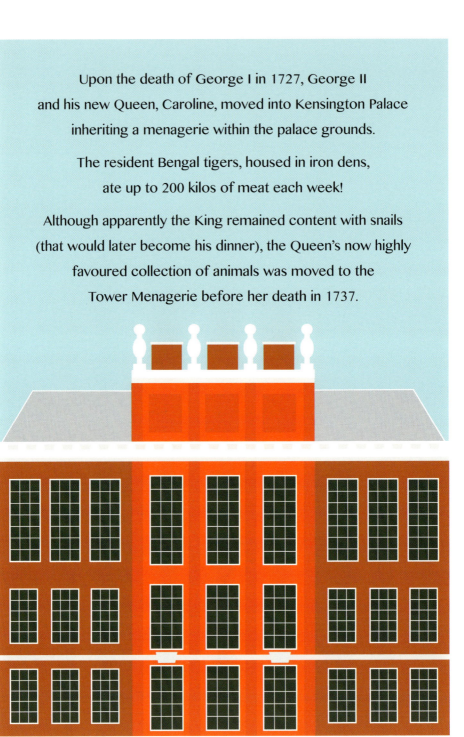

is for tiger

Flanking the main ceremonial gates of Buckingham Palace, at each end of the East facade, there are smaller everyday gates. Completed in 1911, as part of the Victoria Memorial scheme, the Scottish Unicorn sits on the right of both of these sets of gates. The English Lion sits on the left.

The Lion and the Unicorn are symbols of the United Kingdom. They were combined as the heraldic supporters within the full Royal coat of arms of the United Kingdom in 1603 when James VI, King of Scotland, married Margaret Tudor of England. He accended to the English throne, and became James I, King of Great Britain.

is for unicorn

GEORGE & VULTURE

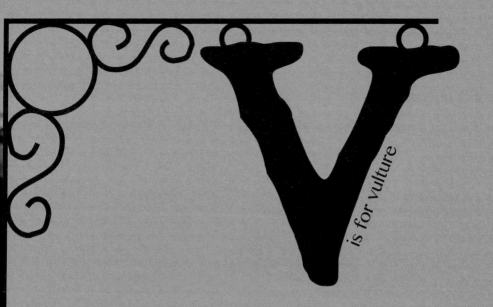

V is for vulture

Established in 1175, The George was originally a hostel for weary travellers. Found in a back alley, off Lombard Street in the City of London, The George has, in its long but not so varied past, also been home to a wine merchant's live vulture. The bird used to sit above the entrance causing much annoyance to patrons.

1666 saw The Great Fire turn the building instantly into a charred shell. In 1748 the public house was rebuilt and renamed in honour of that very vulture. It remains unchanged today, still standing on its original site in Castle Court.

It also famously features as the headquarters of the City Pickwick Club in Charles Dickens' Pickwick Papers.

is for whale

It was a chilly Thursday morning in January 2006
when authorities received reports of a whale heading
up stream in the River Thames.

According to a BBC report the following day the whale
was identified as a juvenile female Northern bottlenose,
five metres long and weighing about seven tonnes.
She was one of the first few of 49 apparent whale sightings
in the Thames recorded between 2005 and 2015.

The whale progressed upstream towards the Battersea area
where she stayed until becoming fatally stranded the next day.

The bones of the whale are now in the National Research Collection at the Natural History Museum joining the 2,500 whale, dolphin and porpoise skeletons already there.

The Xerces Blue
is the most famous of all extinct butterflies,
the last specimen collected in 1943.

Native to the coastal sand dunes of California, it is believed
to be the first American butterfly species to have become extinct
due to loss of habitat caused by urban development: humans!

Some 30 years later it came to the attention of insect
conservationists in Britain that our British Large Blue butterfly
was on the verge of extinction for the same reason.

Grahame Howarth of the British Museum spoke, in London
on 9 December 1971, of the efforts to save the Large Blue
in Britain but concluded pessimistically. Prophecy turned to
truth and within a few years the Large Blue was indeed extinct.

Listening in the audience was Robert Michael Pyle, an American
scholarship student. A thought was instantly triggered – a reminder
of the similar demise of the Xerces Blue. The idea that an 'X'
(a perfect symbol for extinction) could also represent the shape
of a butterfly and spontaneously the concept of the Xerces
Society arose, a non-profit making organisation to protect wildlife
through the conservation of invertabrates and their habitats.

The Society is now at the forefront
of invertebrate protection worldwide.

is for xerces

Y

is for yponomeuta, AKA the ermine moth

Ermine moth caterpillars have their own ingenious method to protect their hard-earned dinner from predators – creating a giant silk web to encapsulate the plant they have chosen to feed upon.

In 2012 an incredible 20ft by 5ft web was spun by
thousands of Ermine moth caterpillars on a bush opposite
Belmarsh prison, Thamesmead, south east London.

Once completely safe the caterpillars proceeded to chomp
their way through the whole bush supplying them
with enough energy to pupate into moths.

Those were some very hungry caterpillars!

is for zebra shark, Zorro

Zorro the zebra shark had always been a bit of a hit with the ladies (lady sharks, that is!). So in 2009, when The London Aquarium at County Hall was attempting to breed the first UK zebra shark in captivity, Zorro was brought over from his home in Belgium to meet his new partner.

Although eager to address the declining zebra shark population this was not a match made in heaven. There were no offspring and in 2012 Zorro was moved to the Sea Life Centre in Great Yarmouth.

Hopes were high. Zorro and his new partner Athena seemed very happy together. However, after producing 18 eggs during her time with Zorro, none of them were fertilised. Before long Athena started to spurn his affections and Zorro was forced to return to London.

the welsh harp

hendon

A Ants, of the super variety, in Hendon. None seen in London since 2014.

B Bees in Victoria Street. There are over 3,500 urban bee hives in London.

C Cat called Kaspar, a sculpture and more recently the eponymous Savoy restaurant.

D Daschund in Brixton without a cafe, unlike Notting Hill, home to a pet bar & lounge.

E Elephants, decorated models for charity. Gold version for sale in 2016 for £2,500.

F Flamingoes living the high life in *The Roof Gardens*, 99 Kensington High Street.

G Gorilla called Guy, first sculpted in 1962, erected in Crystal Palace Park.

H Horse, statue called Jacob. In memory of hundreds of brewery working dray horses.

I Iberian Chiffchaff, a rarity, whilst pigeons are the most spotted bird in London.

J Jellyfish in Forest Hill. First UK specimens, 1880 in Regent's Park botanical gardens.

K Kingfishers at home in Regent's Canal. Also spotted in East India Dock Basin.

L Lions as London's flood warning. But real lion bones unearthed in Charing Cross.

M Megalosaurus in Crystal Palace. Now known to be a hugely inaccurate model.

N Newts, great crested, full legal protection under the Wildlife & Countryside Act 1981.

O Ostrich at the Tower. A popular 1700s fallacy was that ostriches could digest iron.

P Penguins in a designer home! But walking on concrete gave them aching joints.

Q Quagga now extinct. Many attempts to re-breed using horse and zebra DNA.

R Ravens on guard but two of them, Grip and Jubilee, were eaten by a fox in 2013.

S Squirrel for dinner? Served by Zoologist Francis Buckland at home in Albany St.

T Tigers at the Palace. Victoria had a less wild collection: ponies, dogs and a parrot.

albany street

london zoo

the british museum

buckingham palace

kensington palace

kensington

victoria street

westminster

the thames & embankment

battersea

brixt

U Unicorn in the Royal coat of arms. Used by British Government and the justice system.

V *(George &)* Vulture now hosts Christmas lunch for the Swedish Bankers of London.

W Whale in Battersea. Canary Wharf office blocks great for whale and seal spotting.

X Xerces butterfly. Image ID 041828: Natural History Museum picture library.

Y Yponomeuta, a large genus of moths with 103 described member species.

Z Zebra shark. The first born in UK captivity in The Deep, Hull aquarium in 2013.

HERE ARE SOME PLACES, BOOKS & WEBSITES
THAT HAVE BEEN INVALUABLE TO ME DURING
MY YEAR OF RESEARCH:

British Museum
Buckingham Palace
Horniman Museum
Kensington Palace
London Zoo
Natural History Museum
Tower of London
Victoria and Albert Museum

A Curious Guide to London *by Simon Leyland*
Kids Kensington *by Natasha Narayan*
The Book of London Lists *by Nick Rennison*
The Tower Menagerie *by Daniel Hahn*

www.bbc.co.uk
www.belowtheriver.co.uk
www.dailymail.co.uk
www.elephant-family.org
www.hrp.org.co.uk
www.itv.com
www.londonremembers.com
www.nhm.ac.uk
www.parksandgardensuk.wordpress.com
www.petbusinessworld.co.uk
www.secret-london.com
www.standard.co.uk
www.telegraph.co.uk
www.thameswhale.info
www.thedeep.co.uk
www.theguardian.com
www.towerhabitats.org
www.ukmoths.org.uk
www.xerces.org
www.zsl.org

Someone's been a busy little bee!